AF480437

DISCONNECT TO RECONNECT

Crown Phoenix

LATOYA M. GREEN

CONTENTS

INTRODUCTION

Wave makers are those who realize that ups and downs are a part of life's learning system. A journey that was chosen for you is sometimes meant to start alone where the meeting is in the middle. Everything lines up at the ending of your comfort zone… a cycle that is meant for breaking to enable growth in order to find your north node. Anything that becomes stuck, must reestablish the cause and effect to reasoning with its main purpose of existence, step by step starting all over with experience can help you remember and recollect this perspective. Home is truly connected to the heart… where there's a will, there's a way. A saying that reminds you that there's nothing new under the sun even if you feel alone. Many roads have been walked for yours to also make an imprint. You are the author of your story when you choose to take back your personal power and live in your truth. By disconnecting from other's demands and views, you invite and welcome in a version of yourself that establishes a better yesterday. Detaching from negative feelings and anger can also loosen control and allow you to fly to places you may have not yet soared before. "A Time to Heal"

THE DISCONNECT

Peeling off the sweater-unclothing the foundation of **Depression**. *Layer by layer.* Stitched with the *demands* and opinions of others. The weight of the world that doesn't empathize me. Coming off of me, that attempts to utterly overshadow my own being, without any regard to the voice inside, where I am.

Hi. My name is Sarah Lee. I grew up in a town full of **imagination**, where roaming and soaring felt **free**, as long as my true identity was kept to me. See, you can always tell when someone is a **mystery**. Like how her eyes smile without her cheeks, the glow and sparkle that only some can see, without an answered question of 'why'.

What is her tea? Who is she really, behind that smile that frightens me, because it is unknown? Why doesn't she say much or reveal who's behind that unusual glee? Is it her **impeccable** approach or genuine calmology? What bothers her or makes her weep? Why doesn't she show the damage that her heart speaks? Some would wonder…

Time is bothering now, because so much has been taken and used for granted for so long. *It shattered me…* Once, I opened up. Some saw a world of opportunity, so bright it **shimmered** with beautiful and colorful flowers of sugar and spice. They attached and latched, misused and abused, and tried to take over without wearing my shoes. Without accommodating the muse. *That* imprisoned her in her own world.

Making her struggle and fight to create an outlet, to once again spirit-be-free. The demands were horrific to free herself. While others fed up their appetites, to gain and survive, she struggled to **maintain** her mind, back stable in *Find,* like before. Before she chose to open up and share her world. Breathless wants no more. The time it takes to write this is what I want; time for--me, to soar.

Like a fish with no home, how am I to live with no use for my gills? The ones I was born with. *Creative art me.* A **purpose** shouldn't distinguish what is in it for me. I am the acrobat of the gymnast, the reason for it to be. **Surrendering** to other people's conditions is not the **freedom** I yearn for. Although the grant of serenity to accept the things I can't change is a treat, does it still leave room to have courage--for me to change the things I can?

There is a reason for my individuality; what makes me happy is being me all around, not just when and where it placates others. The parts I let be known are parts are pieces that others should not try to own. The numerology of being left out of your own equation: others want to determine the percentage, when I, the owner, had not advised. A start to finish, I recommended; not do alone, but not once did I want it to swallow me whole.

Driven by **passion**, a force by desire. I love to *inspire* when using what I have will take me higher.

Dreams are desire, but mine were sworn, perfectly made for me to have worn. I **revealed** it and created the Born: my design to create the life of my own. No other pens, just helping hands. In a world trying to change my essence, I come to create my own waves. The Jack of none; the triple of all trades. The queen of my world; the last of all says.

The rise has been difficult: the decision to grow within me and not in others' hands. A purple *butterfly* with a brave heart, that's made to love. Also loveth me; put others before, *but now* First. I neglect myself no more.

Disconnecting from unhealthy people and situations, can unearth and revitalize my damaged roots to their natural core. Undergoing retreat is often necessary. One can be accustomed to their own habitat and still want to explore, every now and again to embody the life and joy within.

When is it appropriate to hear me out? It is a crime to be made to feel invisible, when I'm around. I heard them say, "Save yourself and reach out, but trust no man without a doubt." If what I have is **trusted** to work for you, then why am I left out? Sometimes we must take the stand in our own lives--the same one that we used to fight for others.

Obviated from my own realm, a demise of each stem. I now **emerge** to blossom like never before. From ashes to ashes, dust to dust, I cement my upcoming **roar**. Seventeen to twenty, my middle aboard--my **destination** is coming, from one to twenty, from start to finish. I rest assured to be carried in the middle of my winning, oh Lord. Waterbearers don't drown.. planted like the river storm--I rise; I'm found.

Thinking of my morning brew...imagine me laying across the couch, pillow--neck resting, blanket tossed across my legs, hugged tight, sipping on my favorite calming tea. How is it that I could *disappear* in the midst of the sunlight--creeping to shine through the blinds half-shut, not night. I slip through the pages that my pen strokes vivaciously. I envisage all that I have allowed to indulge me--that I have chosen to **disconnect** to awake me.

Finding myself has been a part of my identity. What is my truth? Am I not more than just an aid for everyone else? Where are the stitches for my bruises, the mirror for my heart that smiles back at me? I am no loner; only in my vast conception of **necessity** that is found lacking due to my empathy towards others which in fact enables my humility. But not once for a doormat, does anyone agree.

Where is she, the helper that was left to save herself? Where is the symphony that creates the sound for the fanned ears? The loops that create the strings from the rookies to the pioneers? The course of my being emerged to life. Concluded that, I too have a right to feel loved, be loved, and in sight.

What an impeccable locution to be--chosen a flavor when there are many spices. I have created a recipe abruptly, without knowing. All I know is that this is who I am. She was not just the girl caged for all to adequate everyone else, but the girl caged with a thirst of her own has now awakened herself. Like a light switch that only had to be turned on, I now see where everything went wrong.

Not in the beckon of my kindness or in the just of my labor, but to put forward everyone else before myself, to give where not get back, until emptied--without. Have I yet learned that leaving to recharge, coming back to dish out where I have not gotten in return, will leave me **afresh** in despair? Garnered knowledge to love myself just a little bit more after the consistent revelation was *aborn*. My light is still young; awaiting to shine has begun. Acceleration to yet seize the day in the palm of my hand, my life to make.

May I say to you my dear, speaking as a reflection: Not every plan comes to fruition, but every lesson can be learned. It's not a mistake until in a way it has been misused. Set limits, set **boundaries**, harness a right to choose. Impossible is an understatement, inevitable is more assured.

Do I have to keep myself, when I long for much more? A lover perhaps, a partner of the unknown ashore who lengthens the waves, as there is no house without a home. How integral this must be, the feeling of security adorned. Both pressured and appeased as I air out my yearn.

Days like this, I want to last for long. No longer trading hours in for money, right now changing pressure into pearls. My youth is my happiness. Vital--I harbor her too, where I am fully grown. Every retrial driven with faith is like **retreatment** to **heal** myself, then having to push forward a bigger rock, fighting for something or someone, including myself. Again. Useless when all I see is alone while others gain harvest, create obstacles, or put more on top of my put forth effort.

Every traumatic silence invokes **growth**, insisting whereforth my evolvement of my own. There has to be an effort catalytic to my own, unless I will be left mentally and physically drowned. In this moment there is a revival in the choice to unplug, to insinuate how to lessen my electric bill--the energy that has cost me much more than I have charged.

A girl like her is unquestionably hard to find. Rarely have I one like me.

Write now, or forever hold your peace--is a selection of --find your peace or forever binded thee.

Out of bondage, I flee.

Took some years, but out of ash, the debris, beauty cometh thee.

I say that, "Stress was the wool, the mask. Peel it off of me."

That it was only the *unknown resistance of transformation.*

I taunted me, but later no more.

Had I known the plan, I would not have known the plea; His plan, my answered prayers.

Such an out-of-world, but not obsolete. Some things are beyond our understanding.

I decided to go with the flow aligned with the rhythm of my heartbeat; there lies the truth, no matter what my mind taught me.

Many facets of the different hats I wear are the divergence of my imperfect impair.

Out lining the layers that hold me in stare, uncovers a world I never knew was there.

Presented with relentless findings, whole with me, I define it.

Only when I am full can it be dispensed throughout the overflow, now knowing what I haven't known before.

Can I do this?

I often ramble on. You know, *commit to myself,* what I have devoted to others' calm.

A rebellion to others' **egocentric**, but an honor to my actuality...I plan not, but needed to be. Tempted to answer the call, like always do, instead concealed in **shadow** work until my coming due. As an offer, I remain to be chosen and have a choice to **choose**. Life has its hiccups, but I situate in the moment. This time today, rain accompanies me. Imagine its sound, to (reign) through my ears like a symphony. Two days are better than one, writing in my solitude. Gazing in the air that seduces my tranquil attitude, They say, "I too need my own counsel", but this has been the most impactful remedy I can **vouch** for. Yes ma'am...the feeling is quite ravishing, a creative delight.

Now night takes a turn and I still want to wrestle with the walls alone. Nothing speaks louder than my own perseverance. This here is going to be my lullaby as the sway of my thoughts tuck me in. For now I'm here in a space where my **peace** surrounds. Can my heart **influence** my cloud to seek the light within me that wants to be found? Sunshine and rain, but what's a helping hand with no gain? What I opt out of, I held no stand. Pushing the clock with the *impression* of my return, my eyes won't keep me bothered, rest come...at least for some hours. Replenished like the shower that joins my body. Conversational birds are the only sound to muster, several minutes passed the seventh hour. Holding it together...my thoughts I **collect**. Certainly not, the ones I neglect.

My heart was the reason I fled. It was in **pain**, heavy as if it was dragged along, it was impaired. I remember the day I thought about the **damage**, how much of the days, how long? No one deserves to suffer just because they're familiar to be strong. Strong is what I had to be in order to keep on. I wanted to be kept, but not by defeat, so I decided to keep what was left, to allow it to grow with a sprinkle of love and undivided attention. There are still some things external that are being sacrificed in this moment of self improvement, like music my love. The **quietude** is required, at times I've longed to reach out to the calling that screeches from a far, because that has been my living by far for so long, but was not conducive to my well-being, caused harm.

My heart..are the only words I wanted to say, caught up in a pause, because the thought surfed tears down my face. It needed an emergency, someone to listen without objections, motives or imposed ultimatives. Something unrestricted whole-heartedly so I resumed. Can those do more harm than helpful, make me **depressed**? Shutting out the voice of my own with their rants. I suffocate in loss, I survive giving it my time well spent. In the mist of losing my earnings, I gained time I bought with sense. Using this time and energy to reserve me, accumulating as obtained. Well this is the first time I get to bear how that feels. To be lifted without being broken down in tears.

(Morning Run/Push the pen) This day forward, I begin with a morning run. Something to keep the blood pumping. Sneakers worn, tights hugging, how does it feel to be in a **mind-set**, only just begun? Birds chirping every morning the daylight comes. In a considerable instant, I am permitted to put aside the past. There is no negotiating with my health, it's either *Treasured* or *Trashed.* Throughout the run with every sweat, I release stress.

No good for something that isn't even bad. Toxins out, breath in, just breathe! Back at the door to pillow talk on the couch some more.

When I think about all the people and things I have inspired, this has become the motivation to **solidify** my platform. No one in the world is exactly like you...and because of that notion, it's more likely vital to resonate with the veracity of one's elemental **view**. Goblin time is almost near, but I have had enough fright in one year. How long will this take? Long enough to complete what has started.

Masking an aspiration has become potent to what would identify to my madness. Hope flares even in the coldest facility that circles me bold. Like holding a vision, I focus primarily on the energy that represents me owed. The **counterpart** of a plan that isolated thee. These are the templates of my aggression, I put forward the position. Here I am...demonstrating my significance; *Too I can*, vivacious. My mojo is becoming clear, what floats my boat is now sailing in gear. On my wave...I the captain appear.

A CHANCE TO FEEL FREE

A gift to me, a dedicated moment and a chance to feel free...well appreciated, well **respected**, one I harness indeed. You know what? That vacay has finally arrived, the one I never got and it feels good inside. No more discrepancy of whether my voice is heard, denied. The beginning sound was bleak, but in my actions I stride...a built in wall just to build a stage. **Broken** down in due time, transformant ice-capade due to the coldest days of isolation. I parade the composition of this instance. **Dancing** in the shadow of my welcoming (existence). No horns or bells, but in the pause of oohs and awes...my heart's beating (prevails). A promiscuous approach to the variety of my endeavours. I center myself with eyes of rose petals, in sweet compassion. I'm minding and unblinding my owned world. Convinced that this be the beginning to strengthening that pride frail.

The over-start, begin **again**. Draping up the beseeching sunshine as I deny the outdoors, on my time. The biggest betrayal by far would be, to be lowered out of tranquility that is destined for my proceeding. Creating and **developing** a footing is just as important as being **grounded**. A severity I've greatly pounded. It was killing me to hold on, but even harder when I let go. I was dying, my heart was heavy and fading apart, but I found a way to wrap myself so tight in a blanket of self- love. I've never felt death so hard, though I had to reinvent myself more than enough. As I slumber in distress, I remember the light that used to radiate from my face. Being taken for **granted** has appointed such grief. I can't afford any more losses, like a penny with a hole in it...I'm exhausted. *Worth* more than this, just a polish would iterate the bliss.

My upcoming roar...Grave pain took the toll for isolation, a route I never expected its destination. There is no trip planned, the adventures are in my head span. What is the purpose of this place? To connect with everything that was shared unselfishly to resonate me now in a space of obsolete. Guarded with the memories of what has been, I discipline myself with the acceptation of what has to be. Those events and losses gave the receipt, that this moment was paid for. The future is in my hands. To take back your power is to generate everything sent and **rebuild**. There is a state where the mind collects often, taking in a place to analyze what is soul minding... what is stored. How will I ever hear my voice or write the words begging to be read if I do not give attention to what's being said? There is now an awakening to respire what has been forsaken.

It takes longer navigating from a place of *still*. Mind traveling, pushing the grit uphill. The challenge is to stay grounded until it's rooted. The goal is in the desire, created in the **footing's** field. Even in this secluded moment, I recruit change, a better petition than the one I've endured. By hand, I stitch a new historic, worn with love, mended with my narrative. Chosen to revise what is imperative. Such an impeccable revolution that this pen was given for my future. I am at the point of my conclusion, that my soft **skills** are more than just pure nudity to the attributes I display to accommodate others. It is also worn with integrity and self love as a cover. Where is my substance? Can I not be insubstantial to my own device, but yet mirrored to reflect the ins and outs?

A DEDICATED RETREAT

Rainy days have become often, today it sounds again. The perfect **soundtrack** for the sacred place I couch lounge in. These days...whereas everything has to stop just so I can come in. Here I am...thinking out loud, coursed in my own being, giving time the value it deserves, **unclothed** and remerged. I spy a liberation, such a *breatha* of the one I'm catching right now...is always **founded** to be well necessitated. Stirring in the substance that procedures the constructed **base** that guided my wave. Gone before me as insinuated, "The *calm* before the storm". **Collecting** what comes is intended to be no longer hidden, for it to be written. Many more to come, but my first is right now. It is usually cold when it is alone, but, if naked, it has set a **spark**... "A light in the dark", rare but rarely unsought. **Poetically** unapologetic for what is requisite is also required. I now know that there is more than what has transpired.

Had I not stood for what I am resolute to create? A footing aspired many levels to hold firmly in place. No one ...Nowhere, have gone the journey I have intaked...that is my power. If anyone's counting on me, the once counted out...I am counting on me now with an unwavering freight amount. Where is my **standby**? Somewhere in a desolate place in total **acceptance**, where this is my retreat. Time sovereign, mind incorporated... nice and neat, *Tidy*...to my discreet. A sweet aroma ghostly found in rain, yet it falls and pours with no pain, but confounded to instigate *growth,* where **blossomed** grit is grained. Must I admire such a remedy for a natural cause. I too want a space that centers my *Awes*. A hunting admiration where I deliberately uphold my pause, in the idea that my specialties deserve to be applauded.

Here and now is my take, yesterday was planted...today I invest in me. The future **awaits** my arrival, unfiltered, unedited and evident to thou *Art* me. The truth vast of the bible I speak. A **unique** twist of a plot extinguished for my light to *shine*...deep. For once a path is painted, it can then be followed behind me. The frame was always said to be unattractive, my surroundings...though a *beautiful* picture placed in it. Like a princess misplaced and lost in a fairytale waiting to be exhilarated...*begin it.* The midnight hour felt like a tower crashing down purposely to be rebuilt and **co-created**, with me in mind. True love is finally doing what you love... where you can love it. Knowing patience stirs from identifying that time doesn't need to exist for miracles to occur. It's in that moment, choosing to be...She is...everything I choose to put forward...*Next.*

This is like a simple notary, an **everlasting** letter infused with a sense of devotion. (Note to self) This was the tea I spilled to justify my allegiance to oneself. Had I not gone in, what world would be found...had not lost then? Maybe a candle burn or a spark...Whatever it takes to find home, I thought (I'm in). As far as I can see, a world in her eyes, "Mind indeed". The world I long to create is in me. Classified as musical, the voice within... In the heat it hid no longer as long as I took the job...the one I gave to others while I prioritize them. The reduction of clutter seemed to be more mental than physical, so outside my truth...I dive in, swimming in an ocean of emotions. (sentinel) I barrel **gated** within. Perpetrated to nurturer while I suffered for wind...Now I *just breathe* like a fish with fins.

"Morning Brew"...These have to be my first morning thoughts, fresh awakening. Nothing bothers the order of the day, *rising* from a slumber night. The start over before everything is done and thought throughout the day...connects in time. Clear from clutter and **detached** in mind, the most appeasing moments I can define. How far have I come? I want more... more days where the pages are full. More days where I have arrived. Birth to thought, space in time (Exist). Although I have many accomplishments, it is imperative that I have something solid to *stand* on. **Dedicated** to my solitude inorder to execute and carry off. From black and white of my ink and paper, to color...I come *alive.* Places versus shadows come and save you from a haunted place, not the other way around. A **dream** chaser until my dream started chasing me...*away* from places that did not honor what I was meant to be. Bold and print, I could have been a label, but my many *layers* made it inconceivable to compare.

In a place where voices need no echo in pairs, because its world is boldly whole. You learn more from the thoughts than what is spoken or told (Notice)...that I be the bullet point to this denotation. A World in her eyes filled with magic and space to **create** an impeccable manifestation where future and past are just as important, when we present ourselves... *mind* wide open. Those smokin mirrors are cleared when eye two, become one in near. Am I *favorable* to me now? So much that I see...*still* with sound, music with *style*. Just a summer? I am not...I am **seasoned** to never forget. I remember me now, before the world told me who to be. Before my "I love you" **silenced** me. When two vowels go walking, one is often silent and sometimes it ends with an "E". Can it be *Eternal* or *Evolutionary? Evolving is the key.*

THIS TIME

Hopeful before had now settled to be the answer I know, *reflection* had I become...the anec without dote. In this habitat, I am spoiled with passion and admired by beautiful wind **engagement**. Else nothing compared to the feeling it gave me. Nowhere else had been this delightful. Scentedless *aroma* had filled the air like trees in a breeze this time. What time had me, I plan to give with ease. Had it been waiting for me...it would have come like *now*. Heavenly embodiment with sound...I'm *found*. More days like this, where rain is less than a storm, if be...A **Quiet** storm, the perfect *calm*. If I could control it, I would give it days…smooth-sailing...no parade. I am caught up now to the syncing of my dreams and to the melody of my *being*. **Closer** than before, I embrace the seams of my *soul*. Momentarily remote, but *free* as a bird to *soar*. No other time like this...will I ever ignore.

(**Make Law**) Mind space this shuttle to new heights, a broader horizon that excites. New vision, new moralities, a story within a story...A world within a world of strategic planning and creative design. Pushing the pedal to what rows my boat in mind. Sound is the mover and time is the generator that divides space into present, future and today. When the route you have always taken becomes unfamiliar, a new journey has now begun. My endeavors have runneth over onto this **canvas** of *vouchsafe*. Effort executed the plan now...the *purpose* was in my hand. Normally I'd rest upon the sand, these images I soon to ignite, With the fire burning so *passion* is daring the truth. Make way for all I am and all I dream to be, *end* we once knew...I start here. Creating waves of strides without fear. No matter if doubt creeps, I know what fought cleared...Surviving the night, dawn's near.

(**Vibrant**) Can you hear it? The sound of her footsteps as she enters, the vibration of *your love* in form. Was once mystified to the legions of those confinement...now enlightened. These unfamiliar pages have found to be known quite *contrary* to the lack of *home*. I find it to be a place of residence, property of our *own*. Being present is to scratch the surface, while the future is being articulated to *purpose*. Move while you *do*...even in the vast of times, I travel seated, fasten and bind to the calling of my bestow...more **mood** to go. This state of mind opens many doors, launching to my *success*. Shedding old skin to view in brighter. It's happening now… the breaking of blocks building ground. There are no minutes on the clock, only days and nights. This is captured by weights and heights. The only way to save me now...is through these pages. I *live* now, so fiercely **in** *free*… I live courageously.

Sometimes the only way out is through so I go within. Hear that nag tugging on your soul? That used to be you...until you took control. What would I tell her? I neglect you no more, slow and steady...the chronicle of my **goal,** is forever patched to the timeline of my *role*. Things are changing as the weather *season*. I feel the value of the broken pieces, but yet rebirth to spoken thesis. A proposal...I *committed* to me and departed from doubt, the ultimate treason against faith...**rerouted**. This *image* of me was exposed... of everything I held in deep. Works like *magic*...words like magic, this creative path held the *key*. So often we are reminded...where is the voice gone weak? The one not *counted*, the **lost** in sheep. A lion's roar is all I need..the break down...to fall in me.

I can feel the morning...feels like clarity, new breeze. My dreams needed me to dream. A chatter I needed to hear, longer no more symbolizes a new beginning. My world...the one I would often attend, in the times I needed to feel free… "Soul Free." Where laughter and dance flowed like a river of heart beats. My happy place, where I truly existed, became dreams of possibilities. Only a figure of my **imagination**, because it was *kept secret*. In the outside world, I would put on a cape, but in my world...I would be fully *naked*. Is there an Adam to my Eve? Sometimes I would wonder in these oceans of **emotions**. If I swim far enough, would I find him or would he come "After" me? **After** I've lost and found me "Again". Did I become a fish out of water? Sinking in despair? I realized now that my *happy* place, started from within here.

I never had dreams made of goals until now. I was free-spirited...I would fly when no one was around. I had prayers, secret prayers for all my loved ones to be well. A prayer for happiness, the kind I could have without being **alone**. I wanted to finally live in my world, the one that I would often visit, but this time..not on my own. My dreams were my sacred place, where I would escape...they were my reality only *part-time*. Meaningful aspirations are the ones I could *think* into life, if I had not known earlier, I wouldn't have thought twice. The old void I held inside, blooming like an astro in the night. With thought *ahead* of me, **brought** followed through... with *actions*. I once thought that being normal meant being the opposite of who I am, but how can I be normal if i'm not myself?

A warrior's pursuit...she comes with soul, hearted in gold. I too want to feel valued. Saving my world within and around. There's a subject to the "Matter" in me. Mourning myself...the voice within, I can **hear**, feel... so *speak*. I do it for you still, when I do it for me...brave hearts commit to dedication. I am one like soil, skin deep...minding me. Time is now in me, there is no missing a skip or beat, Turn the world down, when it's hard to cut it off, I still have a mission to complete. Almost there...it's getting harder every feet. A **vision** to build and a goal to meet. A **timeless** piece embedded relevance. Future and present compacted elements. Broad version I now see with new eyes, gazing towards me. Patches of success are no longer far reached...they now stick on me. I can taste the touch like feeling senses, grew strong like roots to a tree.

Untangling threads signified with love that only I displayed and left me thirsty, have now become tougher skin. Where I now feel less cold, more warm even when the thermostat is on. Something new for me was very different, to no longer feel the suffering while others got relief. Like company more stable than obsolete. Have I pushed my *limits* and have taken me this far? Pass what I thought...pass what I have known...to be. I just want to complete, get there... where **whole** is me. My journey to bridge where holes staggered me. Come forward as who I've grown to be. *Pushing*...along the waves, along the days and nights cradled me. In the break that created the pause before the next sound. Steady and focused, I set to break through-- **building** ground.

With thunder being a distraction and fog causing blockage, it was like rain rejuvenated how I can *fly* again. Rosemary like lavender, cherry blossoms like me. Who would have thought that distancing would thrive and strike happier on me. I remember when my eyes used to smile, it was like an inner spark branching off inside me, glowing like Christmas Eve. **Deep** rooted to the inner-me, closed off and guarded, just enough space that I can call home it's **sacred** place. Bonded to no one it was spirit free. The kind of love that allows you to embrace the light for good, no matter what's on the outside. No one could tell it who to be, no one had that authority to take what they did not give to me (*Personal happiness*). Rays to Charles for all the things I could not see, unlocks with a special key with the knowing of every level deserves a new me. Address it with time, followed me to the future of avenues born to seek.

Southern border *calming* tea, my archives to the rivers flown in me. Brace forward...ain't no stop in me. My tears have paved the way, sowed deep in soil ...grown harvest. **Weaving** until I'm no longer webbed, no strings attached. I no longer want to be deprived from blessings, because of my unfortunate to travel to somewhere, so I travel within. Let **anxiety** tell it, I'm no longer in control of me. It's faith turned upside down, powers unfound, be bold in me, the power to save self. That flame that beam of light, yearns to spark. Peak...peak around the corner. Waves around the bend. She'll be coming around the mountain when she comes, the lullaby I held as a child. More experienced **lessons** have been learned. Cipher... it gives me that glitch to temporary shut down. For reflection a serious thought to consider or moderate. Coursing my path...wear it proud, brave hearts are humble.

Sound brings what is heard closer. Mind and ears at work in conjunction. Harmony like **bold** letters. A sense of clarity...magnetic embrace. Feel the move forward, "Sound" so vivid ...I can see the sound move towards me, while I feel it, hear it...make room for me. While I own it, clear it. Touch me louder, if i'm listening... it wants me to...it wants me too. Can I mind my seymour...hungry, hungry to **express**. More sleep would be beautiful, but this is appetizing. I wanna finish...finish what I started. I'm awake now. It feels good...the delicious part of it. Every **accomplishment** leads to a bigger success. Rewarding...caressive...impressive. The finish line is every hypothesis outcome, more wins have not won yet, though my pendants are many. *Back at it again.*

What moves now? Hope is a beautiful **yes** of *faith*, tugging at war limbs while the heart is still breathing. A driver's state of mind into being. I thought about it, but then decided to build it...creating wasn't enough. It was like worn out fabric, I needed to stitch it up. I gravitated toward the shore, the one that would ground me. Long at last I've danced with my shadow, she's beautiful royalty indeed. Worthy of a platform grounded beneath my feet. I stand...washed *anew.* A unique thread built of importance to forming any connections, I made room. Can I see what was hidden in that maid/made like cinderella?

"Absorption": the right to **stitch** my own *pattern*, to make your own marks...clothing my soul. The dry race to finish line without moving exudes it's principles. The attributes to be better than who and what we were yesterday is worth the slow win. There are steps to overcoming which elaborates recovery. *Detailed* in the small successes and most importantly enshrouded in the **progression** you make...keep going. Living is merely not just existing, but learning, growing and creating what it is that you want your life to look like. We have the power...had I not said it yet? This is the secret to mind catch.

Sometimes we are already **living** in the *design* that will build us, but we get stuck in the pain and the **pattern**. I promise not to put a period where a coma goes or an ending where it's just a dialogue that is constantly forcing me with the love I can't see to embrace all that I give out, all that I look for on the outside... When it's what I'm made of. Why am I sensitive like compassion and caring like trust? Pain can be broken into power, if I change it's perception. Fix the painting and **straighten** your crown. In order to grow we must feel, growth sprouts are much compatible with growth pains.

A designed *Quest*, self discovery is merely an awe moment. A **pause** in cry moment, that enlightens and *liberates* a peaceful calm of attention. Had I paid attention to me lately, I might have moved with my mind, those days that I felt stuck, weak and lack of motivation that only left me bound. To come out the way I want, I must travel within. Though the *chapters* are valuable, full of lessons and growth **worn** out. I must close these chapters in order to start a new beginning. I'd be the catalyst for my reform. Thought it, now I sit and listen to me. Turning *negatives* into positives when I add and consider possibilities. If the mind is quiet it can connect to nature. Not just any..a unique **butterfly**.

The detachment was *necessary*. Sometimes you have to close the noise of the world out, go within and trust that those meant for you will be there. Personal development creates a new start called "Again". Stages are floorplans...levels. We can teach people how we want to be treated by the way we treat ourselves. **Expectations** are like wishes, it is important to stay grounded and hope for the best. Traveling through moments that are only made to journey in and not stay stuck is the only way to level up to the next phase in life. You are what you are looking for. Some days I *damsel* in distress, but heroine in every breath. Life *changes* and so do I.

A WAY BACK HOME

I want out now, ready for the world. I want to live out loud. The build up is overwhelming...I can feel the overflow, begging to be released and aching to be freed. There is a reference to this build up, "My cup runneth over". Left alone with no outside influence, I entered me to find the answer. The quiet speaks of loneliness that only finds me, did enough searching now it's time to find my tribe. The purpose was not to get stuck here, but to *harvest* here and gather *growth*. The elimination process has been a **breaking point**, *broken to peace*. I emerge **unapologetic** and honest with myself. Here I am with who I dare to see.

Just enough to remember, but a newer version of me. Why the *blockage* feels more torcherous to complete, but everything I want sits on the other side. I looked in the mirror and she's back, love brought her back. A sound of *barriers* breaking down, releasing and letting go *weight* that felt like rocks, walls that protected fears and doubts. The world she desperately wanted to create was now at her feet. She was alive and no longer suffering to breathe. The focus of other people's opinions and expectations buried the voice that carried her to freedom and *possibilities*....a **friend**.

"Mind Craft"...We're catching up, up on lost times *angry* bird. Spread wings like a smile upon face **value**. Know your worth and every lesson it traveled. There is love in the debris. Chaos brought you home. Centered in a masterpiece. You are what you made of, love and enlightenment...like Saturn rings. Growth is *beautiful*, suppressing no more. What is feasible all along, can no longer be entangled by grains of vines, overshadowing the fruits of mines. Just done, do it for you and do it for fun. Make lemonade sour puss. Simmer up with chin up and brew tea (calm). With thoughts that are felt like hands on me, I get to say yes or no...*Changed* mind.

I still get *anxious*, but this too shall pass, as long as I tell it, I'm **first** not last. Strength in the stems have crafted a new **tale**. Lessons of freedom have worn me well. Why was I so naive to think that it was all over, when I'm only reading from a chapter? There is meaning in existence, patience in truth. Prime to my layers, there's a higher in me that's born free. A *statement* so neutralizing that refreshes focus. Normally I'll be the watcher of my own actuality, but to allow myself to be driven heeds more of a significance, voided in my delight...now **belonging** to the highest version of myself.

Moving past the breaking points...get fed up, not mad. Anger dilutes power while regelation does all the better. Pressure my **precious** jewel, make *diamonds*. There is nothing holding you back, but your reflection, come out the **shadows** and shine bright. Remimick until the morning **speaks**, all night I'll do it again. Find **gesture**...the kind that expresses gratitude and forgiveness for oneself. I'm reminded that nothing is incapable if it begs a beacon. Cautious, but coactive. **Alignment** with what I am asking, sincere attentiveness. Aware that I am responsible for me. It's go time, where dreams come into reality. Once everything else is abstracted, what is the tally? **Me** vs me...the **law** of attraction. Make *joyous* the outer going, the polar **express**. Stitch like *fabric*, the different patches I've quilted, symbolizing the groundbreaking exclusive...the **marvel** of me. It's a stretch that I can afford to take, since I've counted my losses and committed to change for the *better*.

Quiet tunes generate a ticking sound out of thin **air**, and suddenly I can feel love all around me. I sigh with glee, amazed at the possibilities of the unknown, we are not alone. Every *segment* of my mind creates a new dawn. Hope is in the near, but we are the future and the **modeling** is now. Even the birds have come up with a new song to sing...*newborn*. A change caused by fearful times, has shaped a profound and pleasant *flare*. How lucky to have witnessed it, my ears have not been the same since. Major *waves* can cause current events, change is **inevitable**.

Doing what's best for you is sometimes hard, because it comes with an unbearable and unusual **taste**, but if you discipline yourself to make it a habit, it would become the very thing you crave for. Train yourself to do what is necessary for your *soundness*. Build with what you have, for this be the footing to my post. Finally in the center where there is no judgement, but room to grow. Expansion pack, the durability has created an amazing ride. Shooken up cores, but whole founder. My **appetite** is what I make it. An imperfect perfection rooted to it's calling.

Wrestling with the fact that I am no longer where I used to be, but mused to how far I've made it. Pondering this perspective that is now more visible than any words I deposit on to these paperlines day by day. It is *essential* that gravity brought me here. **Purposeful** observation for what was calling me all alone. The occupant of the disclosure is no longer hidden. Growing pains were inherited, but so was the necessary gain throughout the crazy hurricanes. Equipped for the life I *desire*, the void made room for distant love. The calm after the storm. You could have whatever you like, I could have whatever I like, as long as it's what we want.

"A time for healing"…Pass the pandemic into calmer waters. A **relief** of endurance that was once a *hindrance*. Such a foe of survival, but to make it is a blessing we carry. A time for healing deep within us and the world we once knew. Can we have the **courage** to keep going after such life changing? The admissible determination follows suit. *Naked* and cloth in truth. Be it…your will be done. Jump, when your peak is at the tip. **Rise**, like summer out of the blue. As I gaze thinking about how it must be, to finally utilize a voice that was once *hidden* so deep. Will it work the same or need a little tune up? Would it be something even I didn't know I possess?

Where idealist meets logic in the middle, dreams become solid. Adaptive I must be to incorporate such change of events. Pushing forward, surrendering to the flow. How do you know what you want? By paying attention to what you offer. **Expression** is the language the body exudes yearning to utter a mirror effect, love and balance such a harmonic energy. A resemblance of the matter, "I am what I want". To be modest, but with a wild side to balance is less *sweatering* to comfort, layers I distinguished to be either learned, made or pressured upon my skin. Even without it, I am **enough**. The eccentric is one's *unique* design to the world, normal doesn't exist.

Performed a strip search of the version of myself that I haven't experienced in a while. Back to the **basics**, remembering who I am. Accustom to the expectants draped upon me, but found freedom classified as the new *identity*. My drop, the voice over has been the dialogue to my comity. Never has it been so profound until now. **Roaming** thoughts, activating smile, rejuvenates the intensity of the wait, ready for "the wait is over". Here I am, draped in lessons that will enhance my growth. This is love, commitment to ground work for leveling up. Sugar brown and lemons, make a spicy *attributes* like seams sewn together in a *garment.*

Standoffish from being withdrawn and collecting deposits. Accumulating thoughts to process while **adjusting** to growth, *patterns* that are still unfamiliarized, to me foreign. Until I am adapted, this is still a relevance I must learn. Needing it to be, the phase I must **ground** in hopes of **recovery.** The *blockage* no longer lasts and I'm thankful for that, that I can push through when nothing seems to come through. We often get knocked off trail, but to ride a *wave* often puts us back on track. **Dedicated** to the road, I let love guide me. This path conducts a new beginning and I am open to what blessings it has in store for me to welcome.

A DEDICATION TO LOVE

Love has birth a new **dedication**, it is astonishing how love can move mountains and flow rivers with a tough water course. This is the bottom line, after all I've been through love is what brought me here, love is what gets me through the dark times. Maybe now this will be the *thread* to hold us together after detaching what caused to weigh me down. From anchored to floating, I can breathe **again**. I'll swim like never before, "sea" something else, see where I land. A *promissory* determinable future on **demand**. No longer subordinate to the act of my *significance*. I define what all means to me...life is what we make it. Do with well... unapologetically.

A day late over so I work harder, a task times two. Love *motivates* me to **push** even when I feel out of order. **Determined** to create a life I deserve, I move accordingly across these lines. A concentrated solution I pledged to keep going, in spite of the obstacles or distractions I may face. The days when sadness holds a dark cloud over me, I remember I was born at *night*. It is a matter of time for the sun to shine again. No matter how many times the dark cloud appears, it never has complete *power* over me. When the gloom disappears it is inevitable to stronger become, a mystery I am certain to unlock. Hold me steady, vision's in order, the sling be my shot... **forward** thinking and distant horizon.

More time to come, the ride has been a bumpy one...rough, but not passive. The fight has born to winning. Started life in a particular way, to maternalize a new beginning. I think not of the end, but forming layers of events that would never end, **segments** to grow from on and on. A set **foundation** and a chance to start over, not from the **beginning**, but from experience of what I know now. Back on track I ride this wave to the next. Deep *direction* voyaging **roots** embedded by ancestry. A growth in habit balancing the innocence within me for **love** to always be a quality so child-like that darkness can not defeat. A spark that *shines* brighter each and every way.

On board live in color from portrait to bleak. A *timeless* validity never-ending, with a contemporary **relevance** athletic in it's knowing of who you were meant to be. The moment I realize that I am only suffering, when I am not living my dreams. Fresh out of water like baptism, my mind and faith is renewed. With fear pretending to be a best friend, it too be a shackle I must **disconnect** from. Only then **courage** can be born. A border line to disable. Suddenly letting go feels lost, because it's new to my habits, unknown surroundings open wings giving room to **fly**. Faith I say...faith let it be. Let it out to **acknowledge** it and then give myself permission to **heal** (Just breathe).

To gain thick-skin is the formality of harden, a look that appears **aloof**. Sometimes this could be the beginning of self discovery. A standstill graded to unveil its greatest path. The *dynamic* of this attitude is expected by its terms. A **deliverance** so unique it sets you **free**. You are granted this, however you must take off everything holding you back. To unpack build from scratch... In it to win it, but losses perfect it. Hard work makes perfect progression. The greatest version of yourself that exudes positivity effects is illuminated. Faced with the innerwork I must do on myself is the greatest challenger I'll ever have and that matters most.

Creating this life of *vitality* is encouraged by the urge to want more out of life. Accepting scraps for asses isn't efficient, let not your importance be irrelevant either. Move as you must, slow down when you can, but never put a period where a coma belongs in your life. Living **compassion** endorsed fully, let your vision be pioneer...a figuration of the imaginative. Remotely relative while safeguarded I task in my **domain**, with the anticipation of **landscaping** something more fitting to my desire. Concluding with the itinerary to cope and re-energize a more concrete **foundation**.

Structuring is not easy, but it's worth it...you'll never know until you start. Isolation allows life to dissect itself, separating what's true and false, what's needed and what has run its course. Liability is taking *ownership* and account to what you allow and **winging** it where you can not control. Compass has often relay in a form of intuition, *basked* in wisdom trying to make every thought *count*, I am assertive in this moment of doubt. In this **pause** there is a **collective** expectation, one that involves prosperity. Forthcoming event, an imaginable *perception*, a wondrous life awaits in the idea I allow it to be. Fine wine summer sleek, from pressure to pearl... gold iron **sharpened**.

Confined to this space of respiration, to breathe and meditate, inhaling and exhaling while anticipating my next **development**. Along the shore, I allow myself to be moved by the ocean **blues** and tomorrow's **voice active**. Sweetness serenity a *poised* bearing, a moment in time (now). Eagered to establishing the setting in a *narrative* accordance, a boundary that can't be broken. Notated in it's sovereign holds the truth to my **possession**. Submissive and adoring, I **honor** this vocation, Seduced to my own sense of fitting, a *belonging* in people, but self examination. A mountain high backing this thing up...platformed.

SELF DISCOVERY

Back on the **paperplane**, it's an operation that requires *self-discipline*. The reason for this moderation is to heighten one's horizon, Time has generated a peace offering. A firm **fixed** to go deep within, while giving ground. A quiet time to relax while contemplating the next flight. **Devoted** and constant to the **vow**. Rose hearted, the thorns beneath my feet. No commotion, **pacified** to this *privilege* where **relief** is granted, I propose the outcome. This disposition is nature indicating my **turn** of mind. Sunny and hopeful and positive to give **light** with an optimistic **upbring**. Such a flavorable *seasoning*, perceived for it's senses.

Draining every bit of me to be **transformed**, to be refilled with a *novel* and appeal. Feeling **growth** in the tone and every rise above, showcasing a new background each and every round. A feeling you get when you've had too much music, **drunk** in love. A passion that takes **passion** and divides it into **purpose** and a recovery well deserved and *payable*. Divine timing releasing control to live better in the present and delighted about the future is all it's made out to be. Timing is everything and being armed with necessities, qualities and impeccable *calculation*, an *upshot* that creates a better solution.

Making the waves that shifts *vibrations* into sound waves, knowing that this frequency is the absolute speed for this momentum to develop the dimension needed. *Elements* that feature the essential components allows this principle to be well accounted. I **embrace** the challenge, to be brought in **alignment** with self, conducive to my next heading. *Healing* and in my zone to restore a condition of **reinstatement**, I mind the root to make this happen. The author's origin is based in this moment, founded in the break off. A pause meant for bed rest, to give birth to a new start. A developing manner, "nature" and molded **characteristic**.

The **foundation** constructs the beginning, the ideal model and **penmanship** to bridge the connection between body and **community**. A circle of brother and sisterhood, a **united** association envisioned. Backed up and supported...the stimulation needed to be *linked*. All equivalent in importance, as an active engagement is **figured**. Sourceful interest thirsty enough to inspire *soaring*. No presentation without the statistic, no gain without pain. It's pointless to stop me now, a house is built for a **home**. Shield becoming stronger and solid in days, an adulting form ready for a new chapter...a **whole** new world is untold.

You become the **storm** from built up preparation, persistence and sacrifice has **landed** you here. A wide spread of **isolation** has covered me now. Craving for **balance**, can't have one without the other. The teacher for logic founded on both sides, there is no his-story without **her**. Sheltered in bed I come to this conclusion in the attempt to heal the stolen times, the **lost** pages and precious moments that my timeline mourns. Feeling cheated, but determined to prosper, the idea seems far-fetched and forgetting is impossible, but to *recreate* from where we are seems ideal. Regaining the strength to overcome the obstacles are bravery in one, **bravery** in itself. Like a Monday... A fresh week is blessed with a **productive** start to get things done. Train it **responsible** and you'll feel some sense of gravity, *structure* to keep from falling apart. Holding myself accountable, I reckon to *achieve* this day. No matter which way the wind blows, I'll hold it in place.

Positive affirmations are appointed this early morning. A **chosen** matter for raising the veil. Hiding behind the truth has lost its touch, I am now ready to *walk* in mines. This crafty outline is the minding overview self *applied* attending to **own** business. How good things have come out of bad situations, when the odds are against you and faith is your only strength. A climax coming to a head, **crowned** in precious jewel, reaching its peak...more room to *grow*. The impression is **diagnosed** in the footing of this layer placing **firm**. A subjective correspondence imported for *support*. No lack of *concentration* or randomness is bored. Well occupied and caught in the moment, my focus is the heart of the **retreat**. A **chess** piece made for building blocks while composing it's invention representing its *design*...just the framework I had in mind.

NATURE'S OWN

The light of the soul often refers to the spark that pilots the ignition to permit the energy it exerts. Signals often give out warning signs and information, like birds crying in a group setting. Nature can display a chemical imbalance in one's mind where we think this is not normal, but actually it's overworked, overwhelmed and needs discipline...self discipline a humble intake with a compassionate over turn. Learning all over again with the **lessons** accumulated. A *breakdown* on what you felt, why it made you feel that way, what you can do differently next time and how to come over it. It is to be navigated, to be **collected**, reviewed and released.

Common emotions, but when out of control leads to overthinking. Optimism arrives when you love yourself, you tell yourself positive things even when you see or feel pessimistic words are powerful and are filled with *magic*. Give your **permission**, give yourself the advice you would give to others. A loan that is granted when you don't have to pay it back...a blessing given to be blessed. It will hurt until it's *healed*, until you replace it with a **constructive** thought. During a lie in the dark, always remember your truth...what I know to be real and often occurred no matter how I feel, it is *calculated* more than once.

Exhibiting emotional **distancing** has been it's perimeter to manifest an ambition so submissive. A desire so impulsive the *passion* is alluring. A keepsake to canvas and a vision board to assemble. Putting *together* the pieces that were once scattered all over the place has revealed its design *pattern*. An overall balance is an accessible *capability*. This map of motivation has tons of X **elements** for the mind to see. No matter the **distance**, we can still find our way. *Soar* on...and never stop believing in who we are meant to be. Today we are the **future** created for more and mindscaping a better yesterday.

Distractions have been warned. On hand is the engagement I promised myself. A marriage highlighted to replace separation to uncloth shackles and *rebuild* prosperity. A **thriving** condition with a healthy attire. This is a *special* occasion I attend daily. Never leaving the idea that this will open doors to rooms I have yet to be seen. An alternative route was needed otherwise, I wouldn't have moved. You are doing **good**, staying rooted and *determined*. I am not letting up nor am I giving away this feeling of devotion. A vibe so iced in cake, it causes a **celebration**.

Creating *beauty* out of thin air, when all seems **departed**. This is the lost times captured, more brain storming... the wild fire remaining fruit. A conscious **collective** in consonance, a **brave** romance finding it's gestures in deep soil. I waited for these times to introduce a descriptive resort that allows me to *retreat* myself. To sustain the interest. Aware of the seriousness I am fronting the best cookware for **overcoming**. A new reface is in the oven… creating a timeline that was once invisible. It is now being presented to return from lost to form with a capitalized disposition.

With a force so vigorous, I place this manner on a piece. Success is the threat I no longer fear, when *mastering* self success is defined as triumph. A luxury to reinform...investing again...in me this time. Reaching for the stars is evident, finding the peace within. I found this amazing beat that was once at a **pause**, showing me the way, *calling* me back home, releasing the grip of influence and my mind to grey areas I couldn't see before...I come **present**.

A MIRRORED SMILE

I started by myself, I don't want to finish alone. How it must feel… to see the **reflection** of a smile complimented on someone else's face, when I **share** them a happy moment. An **equal** ray of *reciprocation*, it's the little things that confirm how blessed we are. A truth so contagious and transferable it never leaves me empty. I've always wanted a shared moment that would glow us both, from my chest to yours…locked into the reader's words. I can see my heart on his cheeks, an "It's ok" to be *happy*, because I'm happy with you. An embodiment so pure that I can approach it naked and be myself.

Never hiding love when you can give a **smile**, but sometimes you gotta burn a bridge just to create a space of distance. Our way forward is to meet in the middle, the closet **comeback** in *return*. The fact that it is required, approve of its importance. Sharing is *caring*, but so is to **treasure**. A stance in the mirror has brought me this conclusion. It is a clear message and a way to change, the work is to be done inside. The outcome can be a life changer. I want to wear that sweater, the one most fitting for me. The colors are unchangeable and the thread has no limit, custom made and built for its designer.

I matter… we matter when you agree to face self. Self examining can lead you to your north node of ascending. A **better** version of self to occupy your present **foundation**. Taking time to build introduces you to a lot of pain that we once dismissed or set aside. It takes steps, owning and then releasing what no longer serves us. *Reshaping* the way we think can draw a **positive** *aftereffect*, such an **inspiring** development. A source of recognition can be found where the barriers are broken and necessary boundaries are set in place. Mind you and no longer neglect what it is that you have to offer to your own accommodation. Generosity goes a long way and can lead a horse to water.

To be **inspired** is to inhale, "to breathe"... like damn, that shit gave me life! An appetizing appeal that is inviting can be *appreciated* when it is **admired**. A down right essential *shifting* its quarters. The house of dwelling being rearranged to a more acceptable position, the state of mind recognizes. Being **produced** by a feeling of excitement can be a *creative* talent. What endeavors do you aim for? The goal is to be more me and less of what I wore, less of what I heard coming from other places other than my **favorite** place. My sanctuary is my **safe** haven.

SPACE

`Let me be clear...can you hear me now? No one loves **pain**, unless it's the kind of pain that won't break a heart. An exercise would be the idea remedy. A **regimen** to not only burn calories, but stress **away**. Stress affects us differently, but when you *focus* on the little things, you'll find you are too **blessed** to stress. Love honors the soul and caresses the heart, staying committed to what you call love. I'm in love right now...in love with the passion I have for *building* a better life. Even in a day like needing a coffee, I strive when I rise...my new day depends on it. Every attempt is a **ladder** to progression. I am the **captain** of my ship.

Soul growth, the ties of atoms and **elements** reaching from within, turning pressure to pearl, **grinding** and mending. Addressing the fact that I am redeemed and capable of a more lively experience, one that echoes **joy**. A *concentrated* feel where focus is **centered**, you can do anything that you put your mind to. Half way there is better than never starting. Begin so you can do more than just dream, **eye** the prize that is gifted just the way you are. I try not to think about how much further I have to go and just commend myself for every step I take. A **pat** on the back is often needed.

For once I am on time like the clock and its alarm. Accustomed **routine** I have repeatedly set about **tackling**. I have become this behavior, the type of conduct that invests into this matter. With **confidence** I am determined to see it through. No longer a *prisoner* to love, but I remain it's teacher by choosing to hold on to it, even when I feel all love is lost. The lack of excitement for the things that were constantly beat out of me, brings a **depressive** feeling, so I stay hopeful to someday be *excited* about love again. I believe that **experiences** capture feelings and I move forward with creating to not *relive* the sadness.

Feelings in a bottle and a note to self. Create something new and save me from what I've been through. I'll never tell you to get over it, instead I'll help you get through it all. You **deserve** to love all that you are...show up again, this time for you...do it with love and do it with you...I tell myself "again". I can't move until I have completed this task, *frozen* like caught up in time..**capturing** possibilities like framework. Comfortable in my **skin**, wearing what I deserve, right now...I am in the making. No **fabric** is better than what's *printed* on my heart... so I mind that. A Better day is with a spark.

In a **space** of time, **rainbow** hair *wears* me like a **crown**...vision clear, I wore it well. No hair dye...we were finally **connected**; rainbow wonder girl, a **gift** from the divine. **Decluttering** creates a **clear** and clean atmosphere for **breathing** better. To breathe is to see and to see is to breathe...the moments when I am **quiet**. I'd like to come back **finished** and ready to *begin*. A **fixed** appetite that benefits my **agenda** was finally in the mix and I **smiled** with the written on my **face**. Quiet with the talk of **mind** giving a silent speech, a **pep** talk anytime I'm needing the **gab**. Luxury I call it... to take what you **give**.

Space **creates** time...a *timeline* for **new** memories to board. **Damaged roots** I go deep to heal, a **food** for thought. All **courses** are running and I am studying their **lessons** a lot. Until the ink runs out, I mind this **composition**. Full *steady* and **spoiled** with the **sound** of the rain...I *admire* its **company** during my *proceeding*. **Maintaining** this amount of **optimism** has gotten me through the **rain** thus far. The **birds** have beat me to the finish line today, while it's taking me a good minute, the rain's **clearing** has allowed the birds to come out **singing**. The right **adjustments** have brought me up to par, done with **work** now...the fun **beginning**.

A VIBE

Patience sits well with *determination* riding along its shore. Sometimes you have to break your own heart to **strengthen** its core, by allowing the truth to speak **louder** even if it means you have to hold yourself tight and forbid *access* to the lies. **Break** through to break out into the best version of yourself you were meant to find (**Transform**). The rainbow is now **reachable**, centered in my front lawn, such a beautiful view that I have earned. As above so below...A **rainbow** that has *trophied* itself and has followed me home after all the battles I have fought and worn.

No opinions of others should be allowed to touch your skin if you dress yourself...Dress your **heart** and wear your truth like an armour. Some days are less confident than others, but never give up on what you believe in. When all fails, remember that **believing** in yourself still stands...an option that should always be a **priority.** Today the sun smiles upon my face giving its reflection to my heart, sitting here with a smile on my face after noticing the sun *peaking* through the blinds, **blessed** to see another day where my health is no longer declining. Heart, head and soul is *balanced...* an impossible mission that took so long to **manage**, I now reap in silence.

The silent still **speaks**, "Good Morning"...she's saying, how did you like the smiles I put on your face while you slept and have followed you to morning? You're more **beautiful** when you smile. Can you feel me now **raising** your vibration of your **temporal** concerns and *removing* yesterday worries from your hands? It's like they never hurt you, it's like you were **happy** all along. I brought you **forward**, an inner smile can heal you whole. I imagined someone who would make you laugh and played it in my mind...after that, I just figured... "You look more *beautiful* when you **smile**," so I kept it there for you to wear along with your gown in the morning...**awakening** surprise.

Focus on your goals **ahead** with no *interruptions*, we're almost there. Let bygones be bygones and create in its space…an empty canvas will appear, it will be the firm backing of our **framed** surface allowing *artists* like us to have its way, to do it our way. There is always a **backside** to the **front**, a different way of looking at things. Just like an upside down frown is a smile turned around. What if pain made a way to **heal** and broke through barriers to see a way forward? What if *anger* told me to get mad (**Motivated** to make an **Adequate Decision**)? Explaining that I can always tell it what to say, if I keep writing. Be kind to yourself…for you are your most **priority**.

The density of this moment is full of **fresh** momentum. Energy that is being **gathered** to manifest *change*. I vibe in this partake on a summer day. Although time has now **arrived** where I'm still **minding**, I continue with the building of *fractions* that will soon be **multiplied** fruitfully. Shelving a ledge to the wall's building as a **valuable** layer in place. A once **rocky** situation now seems much more announced as it comes natural to its element, a habitat that took **space** over time. It is in this place where I gather this notation, where it is wide awake to demonstrate its **intention**. The building of a foundation *rising* for landing.

A long admiration has now **seated** its length. A successful journey that paraded the idea for **writing** this book put us on one and now vibing to this space jam…headed home. The love from a **distance** made room for who we are now. A *stretch* is needed and a *shower* added to this **moment**, before I move, I want to give thanks to **dedication**. In adjustment there are long term goals waiting that have been **invested** with patience. I'm glad we took the time to flow with *elevation*. Growth is love *wrapped* in **lessons**, some are painful and some feel good. The ones that we make it through, were the *hardest* to get **over**.

The eye within has been patient, but once again **forthcoming** with it's **exposure**. Music is the **bridge** that *connects* to love, a song heard even without playing it's tune. It seems as if I get **more** than one *soulmate* a lifetime, but the **lessons** are what make it or break it. While the **focus** is always on working on love for self first, I resent to grow a selfish love if it isn't concerning **self-care**. A day like **Friday** brings a *closeness* to the weekend and there will be no double standards on what I plan to do from here to *Monday*. My mind is set on **achieving** this dedication...at least for a bit, the weekend has me **freely**.

A **passionate** avenue is being *traveled* where staying a **victim** of your own reality is absurd...**rewrite** the novel. With a lack of **energy** and wind in my stomach to **sail**, I pray for **continuous** endurance. The *excitement* is a **rare** find when every reason is *defined* by others, it was your **passion** that lit **strong** fires inside you, it was love *expressed* from your own *inner* child and It was those **sacred** moments that you dared **freely** and happily... I reflect and **anxiety** diminishes. A homey **atmosphere** I reside in, *cozy* enough to design in...I create from this **canvas**. Some **reasons** are simply, because it's who you are when no one else is **around**, never letting go of the **definition**.

KEEP SHINING

Keep shining your **light**, we can breathe again, let this be your **inhaler**. Let this be the relationship you've always wanted, "I wish I had a friend like me," in *consonance* with the same heart beat, a *rhythm* that rates heart tweets for one not to brew alone, sip **tea** and chime into these times where **rainbows** are greeted at the door, in sync sound in one accord. A parallel Universe where every challenge in life has **won** it's war and has made lemonade out of lemons, many ways…out of **limits**. Never worry about it, close the door.

No time for **unwanted** shade, but the one I lounge in. **Finding** my way back home has built some time in. The birds are always there, reminding to fly again. You are never stuck just spread to **fly** wings. One of the hardest challenges is to realize you're **not** alone, in the dark there are *whispers* guiding you to the light, the light inside you and **practice** makes perfect **progression**. You won't know who you are until you go searching for him and find him in you. The birds **visit** me at night too now, one in particular, very quiet observing not to scare me away. In love with the idea that even I too, acknowledge its **purpose**.

Muted for so long, the only way to *transform* this energy is to get **active**. Those **desires** burn calories, **months** of *stagnation* have gone tired. The lack of excitement is in the gut where clearing is needed. A healthy **digestive** is suggested for a better **correlation**. Thinking of a better performance, I rather **rally** in *peace* with the meeting of the mind, to **improve** its foresight of a more joyful **invitation**. Why get *stuck* in pain when I can paint a sunny picture, after the rain? I want it to be enough so I trace its name back to mine, **together** we are tough and more than competent to *mobilize* this fitting of a **core** part.

A basic *essential* is always intimate for it is the **birthplace** of its decision making and **branding**. Be the expert of your beliefs, for it is your story that can lead experience to inspire. Follow your gut for a more *healthier* **lifestyle**. A celebration of you is often needed to **honor** your core **values**. Be the light where **darkness** has *overshadowed*. Love is **passion** so be passionate about your intentions to vibrate on a higher level up. An **advocate** of *change* is quite healing and alleviating, a jump start to *ascension* is the process of **awakening**. Trying to overcome distractions as I have vowed to *dedication*. Overloaded, I **fight** for clarity and a piece of mind.

Needing stirring…having to summon a lot of discipline and **focus** to dive in deeper. In this space I wallo out of comfort, feeling the shift from all the lessons of growth, in a **space** between death and **transformation** (Breathe Again). Life jackets are no longer needed when we discover the power of mermaids **swimming** in action. **Vibrating** in an energy of **balance** with a *rainbow* heart that is no longer black or white. If you haven't noticed. "we're already getting our feet wet". It was just so tricky, because everything has its own **rhythm** like a cool puzzle and the wet maze finally completes…a new wave and a new day become a breeze (easy cometh).

Evolvement in our new **creation** is an identity alignment. **Pregnant** with our dream, I nurture this perspective. Married to love and a **devotion** to determination, have kept me busy *knitting* my new *sweater* while **wearing** my garments and homey in my **blanket**, like a rose-wooden garden **rising** from the ashes…there are many **layers** to this fashion. Let me mind you and then remind you, to make *passion* your direction, a **headed** love, paragraphed for a paradigm **shift.** To bewildered is just **confusion** while the *inevitable* is hidden to be **founded** in the new lane we've earned to occupy from *space* made *room* for us to **stride** into the next phase of our lives.

ACTIVATED

Driven where I want to be, from a bird to a **phoenix** with more fire and desire. In **spiritual** quarantine set to roam even higher. A **feeling** so young in its old *environment*, it's a turn on to feel the **growth** of soul alignment. Set in **motion** ready to *convert* this energy into power, fresh like new born ready for the next **stage** in life as I outgrow the **clothes** of the old, while being locked into a higher commitment. A **contentment** that took many deaths to be *reborn*. Doing what I want has become a need, the same as always wanting everything I needed. The **source** of vital and livelihood have remained a desperate **attraction**, I now vibe as the precent orchestrating my domain to a new song.

A lucky pause was just the *juice* I needed...to **unplug** and recharge back to the **basics**, my future still awaits. Like a tree holding up the leaves, I've always felt like I was helping others to **breathe**, until I lost my wind to sail from **broken** wings, it was my time to be treated with the kind of love I too needed. You no longer have to **react** to negativity when *karma* has your back, traveling behind your **tracks**. The amount of good you put out is catching up with you when you give it time and space to produce it's favor of attraction (the law of attraction). Forgive yourself for wanting *perfection*, it also kept you binded along with **distractions**. This day has been **favored** and blessed with progression.

Making love to the *energy* that has formulated the words **sketched** from my heart. There is no **entertainment** for the theoretical in this moment, this is about as real as it's going to get, **breaking** down old wall **layers** just to get to love...there is nothing unrealistic about it. Moving with the tides, such **strong** winds coming from outside...a **storm** is howling while I **activate** my pen stroke in bed. Justice for all and peace will decide to join in...ringing in the sky. I am becoming that strong, so many **towers** have fallen and so many of us have *fought* to **find** home. Clicking heels like Dorothy **cyclones**, a system of depression that mended together for passion and understanding, unconditional love *without* judgement fortified energetically.

Pressing my lips against my arm as I rest my **hands** for a second, I thought about **them**...the meeting in the middle feels much **closer** and love is for certain and greatly **inevitable**. The missing *pieces*... am I the one that got away trying to find my way? A creative analysis and subjects to matter, that we are the ones we've been waiting for all this time. *Separated* by **elements**, but **connected** for more. Heads and tales (tails)...the front and back of the coin, but we are *deciding* to see through **together**. Even if we have to fall into each other, a better outcome **benefits** us all.

Been on **powerpuff** needing love to be released. **Without** fear now... today demands **change**. There is a gift founded in the midst of *distractions* when we are willing to see through the *smoking* mirrors, Racket comes to **clear** the way and discover the truth behind those **adversaries**. There is something behind those mountains, we must walk on top and sometimes it takes flying over to see an **unseen** view from a different angle. No matter the *situation*, the **outcome** can be what you make it when we are pacific about prayer and **pacific** about the things you want in life. **Accept** that there are more ways than your own and if you *ask* for help, expect some **change** to your plans.

The **purest** moment of the day is *fresh* thoughts in a quiet place, the most important meal of the day is an instant **unpolluted** awakening before **break-fast**. I still call it the drawing board...an empty *canvas*, this is where the placement starts the **beginning** and start of your new story before any major moments **movements** take place where *memories* and **lessons** are made by our own presence for a day. A **push** is sometimes needed for **activation** and in this moment only *you* can incite the encouragement to propel during a **still** moment. In moments like this, the teacher is quiet and learning through observation, gathering up the pieces. **Ready** to build with the growth and **skills** accumulated.

Each **experience** has a manual, a set of *instructions* for **connecting** the dots necessary, which means everything you go through is important for **personal** growth and self **alignment**. Today I study me, because it is always us against ourselves that need addressing. Are you willing to **practice** what you preach and have I lived it to tell it? It is the roots that need tending to, everything on the outside is just a *temporary* fix. Without proper management there's a lack of health in self endurance. With *patience* and **acceptance** that I am responsible for my own happiness, I'm sided against old patterns that have worn out their **habits**.

A **peaceful** intellect I voted in is more **beneficial** than leaving nothing for me. We are all **important** and made to be needed, but an empty cup can not join to offer. I am changing my life where I uphold to *transform* and no longer *oppose* the idea that I am enough, perfectly imperfect, to be able to **connect** with those that are *seeking* a partner with a complimentary healing **effect**. The first *taste* in the morning always allows you to taste its true **flavor**, after eating and **digesting** other meals you won't get the same taste, you would have gotten before any other **consumptions**...that *sense* goes away, so I mind mine first and **consider** that my voice too is just as important.

CLARITY

In today's addition ...there is a need to *dismiss* and **release** all negative activity that can **dismantle** all the hard work I have done on myself. Keeping my space sacred from less **positive** influence, I didn't come this far to be knocked back down. A jaded love has now been revitalized with **new** life. It's a fun **fact** that let it be *known*, that I have not only earned, but have **paid** the piper for a new avenue to be *identified* with precision, a *carefulness* so faithful in the pursuit of **clarity**. Love is a true **workout** exercising the heart and mind, we can all get off **balance**, stress can cause that, but there is a way to get back on **track**. Cool, calm and *collective*...I am big on **progression**.

The lost times are **recorded** and I am the **leading** lady. A sacred return and **revenue** that is paid with time and labor...a tough grind. I'm trusting the process to come out on a **better** end. Flourishing **xappeal** exotic pressure leading the way to my proposition. It's a long start, but I scrabble to get through. Tied *down* to this **space** until the right *amount* of energy is **created** to make today's impact. By this time the sun is shining harder, later in the day my pen is still **calling**. Almost to the end, just to *leave* time for the next day, just to start over **reflecting** on the building, I **decorate** its unique **design**.

Three days passed and there was no sound of the **birds**, they must have been *traveling*, the **excitement** of their chirps today gives me a jumpstart like **music** to my ears. Knitting the path to my truth gets me up early. If I doze off in **between**, there's an inner **voice** that sounds out louder wanting to be heard, **vibrating** from my mouth and ringing to my ears, a **power** over me too strong to *ignore*. The **urgency** is love calling out my name wanting to **exist** in a time with me, begging for time to come in...like a King to a Queen. Where **space** has taken over, I hear you without turning you on, but the *static* is caused by a **disconnect** between worlds...yours and mines, hers and his, but yet filling these lines before I turn the **page**.

These are no chapters; these are all **headings** to new beginnings. Waves made in a time of a great **storm**. Took years to get this *cheeky*, a lot of blockage has been **overthrown**, removing obstacles from my life. The sun is beautiful like the day I attend to have. Being **breath** back together while being **held** by love, the *missing* pieces have been whole once more after being torn apart for so long. Being broken just to be brought back **together** was the moral of the **story**...even better than before. Spoken words for the birds, I glide on **air-planning**. A mode I put on **mood** that overstayed it's extended in order to put a **smile** on my day.

There is an **accustomed** growth to the **dark**, I've found love in the dark, but it's the light that makes me feel free, an inner light that **ushers** in **healing**. Freeing is **deliverance**, a **formal** statement would be *appropriate* for this liberation. **Free** from *limits* and negative behavior is such an **untying** relief. Nothing's typical about rarity, it's found in **differences** and I am who I ought to be (**myself**). Writing **again** half sleep not ready to wake up just yet, but still getting the task done, the earlier the better. Keeping a **balance** prevents things from piling up, so my *plate* is well **managed**. The goal is **love** and love is a **dedication** I must **express**.

Sometimes we are right where we are supposed to be, in a **lesson** for **growth** to get you to your **next** level. Life is **mysterious** and it needs to unfold. Some things are **unaccountable** which means it's hard to **explain**, but it shouldn't **disassemble** it's factuality. A perceivable **manner** in **understanding** life's part and life's heart is you. We are all a part of the body of the ocean, whether it's bright or blue, **current** events **wave** along and you should too when starting a new chapter in life. Make waves and **consider** it's altitude for an **attitude** adjustment...**rise** above **despair** and **surrender** to possibilities. For *change* is within you before it is seen around. In order to see it, I must first **believe** it.

A wake up call to love, **devotion**, a much clearer aspect ...do you care?

I mind. I mind these thoughts into walking **papers**, a freedom I haven't felt in a long time. All **challenges** are not to be *avoided*, they come out better when they are **embraced**. I look at it as, if I get stuck, it makes me **push** harder to get over the hump, then there will be **greatness** resurrected when I have **overcome** it, like writer's **block** eventually the words will come **out**. A *softer* touch to a **deserted** canvas, I only left it **unoccupied** last night, to rest assured to start bright and early. Where nothing's yet done, I'd like the freedom of the **blank** space to define... my day is what I make it.

I'd like to think of the space I'm in, to give **value** when recognizing my worth. No longer playing **small** where I'll just be ignored anyway. Staring face to face with my **truth** alone, took a lot to get here, broke down walls to rebuild a **happy** home. I think of the path ahead and know that I'm lying right in it as I *ponder* my way to **stand**, to **validate** what is already known. A **significance** to my well-being and a punctuated fathom to my **proper** noun (now). Trying not to get **lost** in turmoil has become a normal task when I wallow in *sadness* of yesterday's defense, but I never **leave** me there for long.

Finally **centered**...everything is reversed **back** to me now, I finally get to spend time with who I've been giving to others. Love fills me back up and holds me to my word. Took a lot of **patience** and *self-restraint* to meet me here, where **mistakes** are not whipped and chained against me or hung over my head to *prison* me, instead they are *genuine* lessons done before I **learned**. It feels like she's been lost in the **wilderness** by herself for many decades and I want her to know that she is loved with everything in me. Stay **dedicated** to your dreams, I've been having them ever since they were given...feels nice to **finally** have the courage and strength to live them. A new day is born and I have just been **delivered**. Such a nice analogy in **significant** respects.

I saw the time he **planted** her face back with his **breath** and she was **alive** again. I guess love truly has a calling, one that brings things back to life. It's time...for the **dreams** that died in you to be revived. Love is more

powerful than I've ever known, it's life, death and **rebirth**...it's a brand new kind of me. I feel a mature come about, and it feels good to my soul. I wonder what today is going to be like? Oh I forgot...I'm the writer with smiles. I think I woke before the *birds* this time and right now they may be chirping and saying, "the **early** bird gets the worm"...laughter is good for the **soul** and I'll bet it does the same for yours.

JUST BREATHE

I can feel the new day *breathing* down my arm, that's how far we have come. Feels like symphony and grace. We have **swam** the deepest going within. Will you look? Your future is calling you here, you won't walk alone. Rescued from doubt and born in **passion**. Fire ignites your desire, I wanna see you now… a beautiful phoenix **rising**. Hope fills the morning, tying parts together. Inspiration is all around you. Jam to the beat of your own drum and walk with the funk…it's your song, your life…live it on. **Brave** strong with the obligation to carry on, how does it feel to be born? Many are waiting to join.

She wore strength even in the midst of pain. Sister frozen **not**…she's melting the pain away. Love can be **strange** when it isn't given properly, for you are mine and I am yours…even if you strayed away. Putting some *ghost* into this moment to save the day. Giving each one the *individual* attention it deserves…**facts**. Daily bread, I make it to quench thirst. A quiet mouth is equivalent to a closed one, It won't get fed. **Planted**…thank God for the rain. The **rainbow** greets you with a smile, a more colorful world. The one you always wanted is yours to claim. Enjoy the life you were given and *embrace* the day. Princess **frozen** "not" she's melting the pain away.

On schedule for today, I made mine. Met quota…**25** multiply extended. You can "bet that" we are cuddling a new beginning, laying close to this affection and snuggled to this **academic**. Owning this time as a crossroad and as a bridge to my chorus. A song lived so far, it never stopped calling. A meeting so endearing …a surrender so **enchanting** was all that I could ever dream. Why must the cat be curious, it's already finding me? It's already finding me. Who am I to Bo Peep? A lost sheep… or a lion's Simba? A *charismatic* approach ringing the doorbell on the *next* chapter. I would like to see the sun after being **concealed** to the dark.

Seeing the world different than ever before, knowing that *change* had to come. A different point of **view** has led me to this open mind. **Tracing** over my mistakes to get the right word, editing right before my eyes. It's really what you make it, no matter how it looked before. *Driven* thoughts can open up the door with new *opportunities*. Promoted by **experience**, you can now thank your flaws and the obstacles that led you to breaking through. Everything starts with being **grateful**, the only way to move without baggage. Sort out the laundry and **wear** the *new* **sweater**, the one that was made for you. Thank God it's Friday.

Making space for time is putting in *effort* towards the things you **care** about. Embrace "matter", because you do. You are a flower bomb. There's a **resemblance** in this day, the kind that reminds you of faith without wavering, no shifting back. It's a careact to providing **essentials** for self-sufficiency. An independence that is no longer helpless or caught up in the webs of others. For some time now, we **battled** this *depression* that kept us **stagnated** and inactive, but choosing to be free is choosing to be happy. A long list that can take you down memory **lane**, but it's in that moment you make change, by **directing** its way.

Making space is creating, *calling* in what you want to give place to. It is empty without what it is created for. An empty **canvas** exists merely for the *painter*. It is not to be debated or **compared**, it is to bring life into what already exists in your heart. Space is **sacred** energy that can't be bought. Patience, love and care is its virtue. A *behavior* that is honest to succeed. Giving worth to its **desire** is maintained with **dignity** in it's grace. Loving what you want, allows it to want you back. When what you want, wants you...it is because you have mirrored and preserved that **effect**.

FROM THE MUSCLE

Every **experience** has *built* you from the muscle with no regrets. Utilizing the biggest muscles is what takes you up the **ladder**. Strength, grit, courage, perseverance, humility, experience and observation…each play an important role for the *desire* of true **contentment**. What do we do when all we've known was to look for our other half, but then we become **whole** after being **broken** to peace? Maybe that's the next level of **cake layers**. We all look for something that our soul finds missing, but can it desire someone who has also done a mission? A creative **hunger** that unites a twin flame. I guess it's true, sometimes we are "meant for more".

Self-discipline plays a major part in *digesting* the journey. Moving through a still stand has been its biggest **challenge**. Mind over matter won't mind. A temporary **halt** just to examine possibilities, to build with the scraps that were once buried for these times. There are no obstacles in this space, for it has me for its shape. The right **direction** is in the center, being **grounded** takes you places you were meant to go. Wild flower how many colors would you like to explore? I say this…with no longer an upside down smile, that I have contoured to fit my own face gesture, by *deciding* to **face**… it right side up.

You don't have to try so hard all the time, your natural energy should draw in your tribe, it's a **vibe**. Go hard when necessary, but being yourself is free as love. Why are the *birds* sounding like cats during this off and on rain? Or is it that we all sound the same when we are scared or just want to be loved? A *cry* out that is **demonstrated** in different ways. Some show how they want to be treated by the way we treat others, but when this is not reciprocated, this is when it should be reflected upon your reflection, not the one in the mirror that is solid, but inward where your soul lives.

Freedom is giving yourself permission to be all that you ever wanted and not holding anyone else accountable.

Just do...This is the time we *marvel* at how far we've come. In the **distance** between yesterday, I welcome you to **X-Paradise**...where being out of your comfort zone can bring you new comfort, new ideas and a new breath of life. There is a *destination* approaching, It's not final, it's actually brand new. An empty *heading* ready for **action.** Have you ever wanted to go back to the future, what if you and your new **sweater** was a part of this *future*, would you wear it now? I ask myself...when will it be the right time? Why not start now? This is a **reference** I can refer back to as an extended version, while making waves to the songs, I haven't **written** yet.

Get up... wake up, time is here now, you've been waiting for a sign. Look, even the *birds* have **frozen** now...all in a **cocoon.** Nothing left, but a sound of a pen drop. Everything is ready to hatch, like a *purple* butterfly. They're in line, everything is waiting to be *transformed*, change is in the air. Get rid of all the fog, no more smoking mirrors. Time has been **preserved** waiting for life to begin. Seems as if I was always ahead, so I've been waiting on time to catch up. The numbers have gone up and down and then. There was a **standstill** of all the birds. A non creative world with no color just grey fog...everything hanging upside down, side by side waiting to be reborn, waiting to be created and woken up. A picture to **repaint.** Get up, wake up, this is the next page you've been searching for. I have found it...in a dream.

A scary scene left to be continued...Real life controls the dreams now. A time when **superheroes** of all kinds are needed. Arts and crafts and so many helping hands. The kind of **inspiration** needed to inspire our **storyline.** Is it the born or the **co-creators** of the universe? I'd expect it was a stitch to my sweater. What kind of power is there in truly being yourself? Are there super capabilities? I ponder as I lie awake now. My ship has come in now. Even in the **disconnect**, the right things have always been **connected**, it took a disconnect to find it deep within. Some have always been there, some were meant to be *discovered*. We have always had the power to create the life we desire. I have told my mind that this was my story, *poetry*, philosophy and then it was ours. I wonder what life could be if I honor my hard **work** and begin *wearing* my new **sweater.**

We made it, in the blank space I've been waiting for...the **distance** between here and now. The next *segment* is full of blank pages. Caught in the **frozen**, I choose to come alive, to no longer live in a portrait, but to make waves that are sound. **Pregnant** with possibilities have reached full term. My water has broken in order to break the ice. I arrive as the **author** and no longer the *ghost* writer, ready to start right at the end, the end of a *stalemate*... and look what I'm **wearing**! The new sweater I learned to stitch during the course of the pandemic, a gifted talent I discovered I had deep within my skin... "**Unraveled**". A meeting in the middle has met a connection and wise understanding that everything has a song, a **voice** even without a sound...a name that long to be heard. Present, I yield to the *calling*, free as a bird. Where *paths* can meet and weather the storms. My belongings have found "I"...with an **embrace** that **fits** well.

Learning to shut doors in order to walk in new ones, has not been easy, but I learnt that nothing worth having isn't always easy. I now realize the true meaning and behind my constant display of 25 **multiply**. Although it has clearly been a road map of *motivation* for me, it has been a *surpassing* goal. With that being said, the shuttle is ready to lift off. A never ending dynamic rooted in its **grounding**. Be reminded that nothing is free in life, not even the worth that's founded in you, it is earned and accepted. You be the first... I mind my own business to shape its **structure**, to *breathe* with the wind "Up" built my empire. A **process** that impetrated the work...I called it "**Whoa**"!

* God, grant me the serenity to accept the things I cannot change, courage to change the things I can, and wisdom to know the difference. "The Serenity Prayer" written by, The American theologian Reinhold Niebuhr